Riding
with
Aunt Lucy

by Sharon Phillips Denslow

Pictures by Nancy Carpenter

Bradbury Press New York
Collier Macmillan Canada *Toronto*
Maxwell Macmillan International Publishing Group
New York Oxford Singapore Sydney

A NOTE FROM THE ARTIST

The illustrations for Riding with Aunt Lucy *were drawn with soft pastels on Fabriano Artistico watercolor paper. The slightly rough texture of the paper allows me to build layers of color. You can see evidence of this if you look closely at some of the pictures. The finished illustrations were color-separated and reproduced using four-color process.*

The picture of Edgar on the jacket flap was drawn by
Tracy Mrowca, age eight, of Rocky River, Ohio.

Bradbury Press
Macmillan Publishing Company
866 Third Avenue
New York, NY 10022

Collier Macmillan Canada, Inc.
1200 Eglinton Avenue East
Suite 200
Don Mills, Ontario M3C 3N1

First American edition
Printed and bound in Hong Kong by South China Printing Company (1988) Ltd.
10 9 8 7 6 5 4 3 2 1

The text of this book is set in Century Book.
Book design by Julie Quan

LIBRARY OF CONGRESS CATALOGING-IN-PUBLICATION DATA
Denslow, Sharon Phillips.
  Riding with Aunt Lucy / by Sharon Phillips Denslow ; illustrated by Nancy Carpenter. — 1st American ed.
       p.   cm
    Summary: On drives with his friend Leonard's great-aunt, Walter never knows what the trio will discover.
    ISBN 0-02-728686-X
    [1. Travel—Fiction.   2. Great-aunts—Fiction.] I. Carpenter, Nancy, ill. II. Title.
PZ7.D433Ri   1991
[E]—dc20   90-37803

For Lena Cole Phillips,
and Edith Canup Riley,
my grandmothers
from Benton, Kentucky,
who never learned to drive
and never got to have adventures of their own,
and to Mama and Daddy,
who always let me have the car.

—S.P.D.

For Nana and Grandy
—N.C.

When school is out for the summer, Leonard and I go with Aunt Lucy on her exploring trips. She says we are the only two people she knows who like riding around as much as she does.

Aunt Lucy is Leonard's great-aunt. She is seventy years old, but she has only been driving a car for eight years.

Aunt Lucy takes her old blue Chevy out for a drive almost every day. She says she is making up for lost time.

We are going riding with Aunt Lucy today.

"I think you boys should meet Edgar," Aunt Lucy says.

"What road does Edgar live on?" Leonard asks. Leonard is in charge of our maps. He marks the roads we go down and draws in unmarked roads we find, so that his map is full of squiggly lines snaking across it.

"No End Road," Aunt Lucy says, "off of 68, to the south, between Olive and Fairdealing."

"It's not on here," Leonard announces after surveying his map. When we get there, he will draw it in, adding curves and hills and bridges that we find.

I keep the logbook. In it there are names of people we've met, names we liked on mailboxes and signs, places that have good chili dogs, flowers and birds and trees and animals we've seen, roads we will never travel again, and our favorite roads.

Kirksey Road is there. That's where I sat down in poison oak at the Ford Cemetery, where Aunt Lucy's grandfather—that makes him Leonard's great-great-grandfather—a Civil War soldier, is buried.

Nailhead and Pie are in the logbook, too.

Nailhead is a starling that we found hurt in the middle of Sledd Creek Road. He still can't fly and sits in Aunt Lucy's apple tree waiting for us to feed him.

Pie is a big calico cat. When we found her, she was a kitten. She had been left in a shoe box on the side of Jackson School Road. Pie brings garter snakes to Aunt Lucy all summer.

The first page of the logbook is also Aunt Lucy's checklist. She makes me read through it every time before we leave.

"Gas?" I begin.

"Check. Full tank," Aunt Lucy answers.

"Wipers, headlights, taillights, turn signals, tires."

Leonard runs around the car checking while Aunt Lucy pushes buttons and pulls levers. "Check, check, check, check, check!" he shouts.

"Horn."

Aunt Lucy blasts the horn. "Check."

"Map."

Leonard grins at the impossibility of him ever being without his maps. "Check!"

"Water. Lunch. Caramels. First-aid kit. Flashlight. Blanket. Field glasses. Boots. Camera."

All of these things are ready to be piled in the backseat. Aunt Lucy likes to be prepared.

Then we are finally on our way.

We pass my house and beep even though my parents are at work and no one's there except Elmo, my cat. We pass Leonard's house and beep at his mother.

"What's Edgar like?" I ask.

"You'll see" is all Aunt Lucy will say.

No End Road is a hilly road. It's the kind we like, where we can't see too far ahead so there's always the possibility of something waiting to surprise us.

We pass a store with a pop machine and one gas pump out front and a sign over the door that says

MAYBELLINE'S

We keep going up and down two roller-coaster hills, then around a honeysuckle-lined curve...

...until we stop in front of a farmhouse.

Aunt Lucy beeps three times and we watch the front door, expecting Edgar to come out any minute.

Behind the house by the barn, a farmer in a cowboy hat waves and opens the gate.

"There he is!" Aunt Lucy exclaims.

A big pig dashes through the gate and, grunting and squealing, runs toward us.

"Walter, Leonard, meet Edgar," Aunt Lucy says, laughing at our amazed faces. "Better open the door and let him in."

We are not fast enough. Edgar rushes up to the
car and sticks his big wet nose in the window.

When we finally get the front door open
Edgar pushes by us, snuffling, and clambers up
onto the seat, where he sits on his fat haunches,
ready to go.

"Is he really going with us?" Leonard asks.

"For a little ways," Aunt Lucy says.

"Can I pet him?" I ask.

"Sure," Aunt Lucy says. "He likes having his head scratched, and his back, too."

Edgar has coarse, bristly hairs and long, black eyelashes. As I scratch, he grunts and rolls his wise eyes in my direction.

"How did you meet him?" Leonard asks.

"Last spring when I was taking a drive to admire the dogwood down through here, there was Edgar standing by the road, looking wistfully up and down as if he were expecting someone. Turns out every Monday Maybelline picks up Edgar and takes him for a ride to the store. Well, Maybelline couldn't come, so I offered to take him myself, and Edgar and I have been friends ever since."

"Why doesn't the farmer take him?" I ask.

"Mr. King? He's got bad eyes," Aunt Lucy answers.

"Why doesn't Edgar just walk to the store?" Leonard asks reasonably.

"What?" Aunt Lucy says, petting Edgar on the shoulder, "and miss out on his car rides? Edgar's too smart for that."

When we get to the store, Edgar runs up to the screen door, grunting and squealing.

"Hold your horses, Edgar, I hear you!" a woman shouts back. She comes out with a tin pan, a big bag of cheese curls, and a bottle of chocolate pop.

"Hello, Lucy. I see Edgar's got two new friends."

"Maybelline, this is my niece's boy Leonard and his friend, Walter," says Aunt Lucy.

"Pleased to meet you," Maybelline says, dumping chocolate pop and a pile of cheese curls into the pan. Edgar plows right in, spraying cheese curls everywhere and getting yellow crumbs all over his snout and eyelashes.

"Cheese curls?" Maybelline asks, handing us the half-empty bag.

When Edgar is finished, we all pile back in the car, wave to Maybelline, and head out. When we reach Edgar's house, Aunt Lucy beeps the horn and sails by.

"Edgar likes a little bit of a ride," Aunt Lucy says. "Besides, you need to see why No End Road is called that."

About two miles from Edgar's house, the road
makes a circle around an old graveyard on a hill and
doubles back to connect up with itself again.

"Neat," Leonard says. He draws a loop on his map.

Edgar refuses to get out of the car when we get back to his farm. But then Mr. King whistles, and Edgar hurries to his friend.

"Call me if Edgar needs a ride next Monday," Aunt Lucy hollers.

Mr. King waves his hat in acknowledgment.

I discover a couple of Edgar's bristly hairs on the seat and find some tape in the car pocket and tape the hairs in the logbook. Beside them I write, "Gave Edgar a ride today to Maybelline's and No End Road."

"Well, boys," Aunt Lucy says, "we've finally found someone who likes to go for rides as much as we do!"

And we all laugh and have a caramel in Edgar's honor.